NATALIE SAVVIDES

MEET THE HEARTBEATS

AUSTIN MACAULEY PUBLISHERS™
LONDON • CAMBRIDGE • NEW YORK • SHARJAH

Dedication

For all children everywhere...

Let's try to make the world a happier place!

The Heartbeats are a family that are happy and kind,
They love adventure and the fun things they find.
Whatever they do, they do with care,
Not just at home but everywhere.

Hattie, Harry, Henry and Henrietta,
Live with kindness to make life better.
'It's cool to be kind' is their message to you,
Use it please if it's all that you do!

Grandma and Grandad, Uncle and Aunt,
Kindness grows from every seed they plant.
There's a lot to find out about this funky crew,
And tons to learn from all that they do!

Aunt Alice has a special friend Fay,
Happily they go about their day...
Baby Heartbeat is in their care,
Causing michief everywhere!

And then there are friends that are like family,
Wilf, Cameron, Kim and Abi,
All so different - but equally kind!
Inclusion and acceptance, helps everyone shine!

Dipsy the dog and Coco the cat,
Add to the adventure wherever they're at!
The Heartbeats' pets are full of surprises,
Amusing everyone with all that arises.

The Heartbeats rock in their quirky ways,
Living and loving, in a happy haze.
They know the key they know the answer,
It's kindness that's the link to laughter.

Let's be happy and follow their example,
And make the world we live in truly sparkle.
Being kind to each other, to ourselves and the planet,
Can't hurt at all, honestly... can it...?

We learn from Henry, Henrietta, the wider family too,
Heartsville flourishes with the things they do.
The atmosphere's fantastic at Heartsville High,
The Heartbeats are there - that's why!

It's cool to be kind don't forget don't forget,
Choose it and use it as a very first step.
You'll love it, you will, I promise you'll see,
We'll all be happy, every, you and me!

It's **Cool**
to be *Kind*

About the Author

Natalie is a mother of two young children passionate about making the world a kinder, happier place for children to flourish in. She created The Heartbeat family as a tool to facilitate the education of kindness to the youngest generation with Henry & Henrietta Heartbeat as the two main characters spreading the message of kindness through example. The books are simple, fun and easily understandable enabling children to learn and enjoy the importance of kindness and how to action it in daily life.

ISBN 9781528995535 (Paperback)
ISBN 9781528995542 (Hardback)
ISBN 9781528995559 (ePub e-Book)

www.austinmacauley.com

First Published (2020)
Austin Macauley Publishers Ltd
25 Canada Square
Canary Wharf London
E14 5LQ